FIRST HE MADE THE SUN

By Harriet Ziefert

Paintings by Todd McKie

G. P. Putnam's Sons • New York

First He made William,
then He made Nathaniel
—H.M.Z.

For Jesse
—T.M.

Library of Congress Cataloging-in-Publication Data
Ziefert, Harriet. First He made the sun / by Harriet Ziefert;
illustrated by Todd McKie. p. cm. Summary: Presents a rhyming rendition of the
six days in which God made the seas, the skies, and the creatures and of the
seventh day on which He rested to admire them. [1. Creation Fiction.
2. Stories in rhyme.] I. McKie, Todd, 1944- ill. II. Title.
PZ7.Z487Fir 2000 [E] –dc21 99-27020 CIP
ISBN 0-399-23199-4
1 3 5 7 9 10 8 6 4 2
First Impression

First He made the sun,

And then He made the moon.

Then He made the possum,

And then He made the 'coon.

He made all the creatures,
Made them one by one,

Put them in the sun to dry
As soon as they were done.

He made fishes, clams, and oysters,
But they dried out in the breeze,

So He sprinkled them with water
And put them in the seas.

He saw the skies were empty,
But He knew what to do.

He made the birds who fly so high
And chirp and tweet and coo.

The great, flat sandy desert
Was the hottest place He made.

Joshua trees and cactus
Gave snakes and lizards shade.

He made the mighty jungle
Thick with everything.

Lions and tigers hunted;
Monkeys learned to swing.

He made some creatures furry,
And some He made with scales.

He created fields and forests
With bears and snakes and snails.

Adam was the First man
That the good Lord blessed.

Adam named the animals.
Which ones do you like best?

The seas, the skies, the creatures—

God made them one by one.

On the seventh day He rested
And admired what He'd done.

Author's Note

I was initially attracted by the first few lines of the traditional African-American folksong "First He Made A Sun" in the book *Sing It Yourself: A Collection of Folk Songs* edited by Dorothy Gordon, published by E. P. Dutton in 1928. The song makes a number of other appearances in collections of traditional spirituals, with different variations on the verses. I wanted to elaborate on those first few lines to create a complete story in the hope that the words and spirit of the original would find a new life in a picture book for young children. As I expanded on the original, it became clear that this version of the creation myth would be unique.

—*Harriet Ziefert*